Max the Mighty Superhero

by Trina Wiebe

Illustrations by David Okum

Lobster Press ™

Max the Mighty Superhero
Text © 2003 Trina Wiebe
Illustrations © 2008 David Okum

Published in 2008 by Lobster Press™
1620 Sherbrooke Street West, Suites C & D
Montréal, Québec   H3H 1C9
Tel. (514) 904-1100 • Fax (514) 904-1101 • www.lobsterpress.com

Publisher: Alison Fripp
Editor: Kathryn Cole
Graphic Design & Production: Tammy Desnoyers

We acknowledge the financial support of the Government of Canada through the
Book Publishing Industry Development Program (BPIDP) for our publishing activities.

We acknowledge the support of the Canada
Council for the Arts for our publishing program.

The Canada Council | Le Conseil des Arts
for the Arts | du Canada

Library and Archives Canada Cataloguing in Publication

Wiebe, Trina, 1970-
	Max the mighty superhero / by Trina Wiebe ; illustrations by David Okum.

(Max-a-million, ISSN 1701-4557 ; 2)
ISBN 978-1-897073-95-7

	I. Okum, David, 1967- II. Title. III. Series: Wiebe, Trina, 1970-
Max-a-million ; 2.

PS8595.I358M393 2008		jC813'.6		C2008-901093-0

Printed and bound in Canada.

Text is printed on Rolland Enviro 100 Book,
100% recycled post-consumer fibre.

Table of Contents

1 **Men in Tights**

"Little Simon Tuttle was returned safe and sound to his frantic parents today," announced the perky television newscaster. *"A one-thousand-dollar reward was presented to the child's rescuer, who discovered the toddler sleeping peacefully in the gorilla enclosure at the City Zoo. Apparently Simon had wandered away during a family outing. In other news . . ."*

"Boy, I wish I had a thousand bucks," said Max. He slumped back on the couch and flipped through the channels so fast they blurred. Commercials, commercials, and more commercials. Finally, he spotted his favorite Saturday morning cartoon show.

"Rats," he muttered. "I've seen this one a hundred times." He lifted his finger to change the channel again, but then he stopped.

A cartoon superhero with slicked back hair and mega-sized muscles zoomed across the sky.

He smashed through the side of a brick building and single-handedly defeated an evil gang of bank robbers. The handsome hero grinned, the townspeople cheered, and the mayor presented him with an enormous solid gold key to the city.

"A superhero," Max said slowly. He stared at the screen without seeing the commercial for glow-in-the-dark sugarcoated breakfast cereal. His brain buzzed, the way it always did when he got one of his wonderful ideas.

A missing child found.

A bank robbery thwarted.

What did these two things have in common?

"Jumping justice-fighters!" Max cried. He leaped off the couch. "Why didn't I think of it sooner?"

Max tossed the remote aside and raced to the kitchen, where he found Mom on the floor surrounded by dozens of little glass jars.

"Hi, sweetie," she said, looking up from the small black machine she was holding. "I decided it was high time I labeled and alphabetized my spice jars. With the help of the Label-Meister 3000 I'll be able to tell at a glance if I'm running low on cinnamon or paprika or . . ."

"That's great, Mom," interrupted Max. "Listen, can I go over to Sid's house? I've had the most fantastic idea!"

Max knew it was rude to interrupt, but sometimes it was the only way to get into the conversation around here. Dad was a reporter for the Brooksville Times, and Mom worked part-time at the local library. They didn't ignore him, exactly, but when Dad was working on a story or when Mom was in the middle of one of her projects, they seemed to forget all about the world around them. Including Max.

"There's nothing like a neatly labeled spice cabinet," continued Mom. "I just can't decide on the lettering. I thought perhaps something fancy, but then I wondered if I should use a simpler font with a pretty border instead."

"Yup, great, definitely the border," agreed Max. He jiggled impatiently, trying to catch Mom's eye. "Guess what? I've decided to become a superhero. Not the kind that wears tights and flies through the air," he said before Mom could laugh at him. "But the kind who rescues people and does good deeds."

"Great, honey," said Mom, tapping at the Label-Meister 3000's miniature keyboard. "Have you had breakfast yet?"

"I'll grab something at Sid's house," said Max. He was too excited to eat now. This new idea could be the one that finally made him rich.

Max had always known he was meant to be a millionaire. He knew it instinctively, like he knew he'd love to cross the desert in a hot air balloon and he'd hate to eat deep-fried octopus tentacles. He already had a wealthy-sounding name. Maximillian J. Wigglesworth III. All he needed was the money to go with it.

"Can I go?" he asked again. "I really need to talk to Sid."

Mom clicked the print button. "I guess so."

Max grinned and headed for the door. He was halfway there when Mom looked up with a puzzled frown. "Did you say something about needing tights?"

Max sighed. "No, Mom."

She shook her head and turned back to the Label-Meister 3000 as it pleeped and whirred and spat out the first label. "Okay, then, have a nice visit. Say hello to Mrs. Stubberfield for me."

"I will," called Max. He pushed open the door and leaped down the front steps, anxious to tell his best friend his new plan.

It was genius. It was foolproof. And it was going to make him the richest boy in Brooksville!

2 Zucchinis and Superheroes

Sunflower seeds crunched under Max's sneakers when he reached the Stubberfields' gate. A bird squawked and flew to a nearby telephone pole, where it watched Max walk up the rock path to the house.

Birdfeeders and popcorn strings and giant pinecones slathered in peanut butter hung everywhere. Sid's parents, Bliss and Ziggy, liked to feed birds. They liked to feed squirrels, too. And butterflies and bees and anything else they could entice into their yard. The grass was tall and weeds were allowed to flower, making the environment more attractive to Mother Nature's creatures. Max thought it looked interesting, but Sid, and quite a few of their neighbors, thought it just looked messy.

Max reached for the metal woodpecker doorknocker and rapped twice. After a moment the door opened.

"Hey dude," said Ziggy. His feet were bare and his red, shoulder length hair was pulled back in a loose ponytail. "Looking for Sid?"

"Yup," Max nodded, peering into the house. "Is she here?"

Ziggy shrugged and stepped aside to let Max in. "She's probably out back. If you find her, let her know I'm looking for her."

"Okay," said Max. He walked through the funky purple and orange living room, with its lumpy tie-dyed beanbags instead of sofas and chairs, down a hall, and out the back door.

The Stubberfields' backyard was even wilder than their front one. Ziggy worked on his art here, oversized sculptures made from other people's discarded junk, like lawnmower parts and old propellers.

Max made his way to the back corner of the yard where Sid's tree house was, stepping carefully around a rusty car fender and avoiding a pile of mattress springs. He stopped at the base of a large maple tree and squinted through the pointy green leaves.

"Dippy? You up there?" he called.

A head covered in pumpkin-colored curls appeared in the tree house doorway. "I told you to stop calling me that."

Max grinned. Sid's real name was Serendipity Sunshine Stubberfield, but she detested it. Max had sworn a blood oath that he'd never reveal her secret to anyone. He thought Sid suited her much better, anyway, the way she always wore blue jeans and scuffed runners and had a Brooksville Batters cap permanently pulled down over her eyes. Still, he liked to tease her once in awhile.

"Sorry," said Max. "Can I come up?"

"Hold on," said Sid. She disappeared for a moment, then tossed down a sturdy rope ladder. Max jumped, caught the lowest rung, then hauled himself up until his head poked through the tree house floor.

Unlike the Stubberfields' house, Sid's tree house was plain. Plain wooden walls plastered with baseball posters, a plain milk crate for a table, and a plain shelf in the corner loaded with comic books and Sid's secret supply of candy and gum. Not a bead, fringe or peace sign anywhere.

Max climbed in and sat with his back against the wall, his legs dangling through the hole. "Whatcha doin'?"

Sid shrugged. "Hiding. Ziggy wants me to help him weed the zucchini patch. When you don't use chemicals, the weeds can get pretty big."

Max grinned. "Listen, I need your help. I've had the most wonderful idea."

Sid pretended to yawn. "Another one? Every week you come up with a get-rich-quick scheme. And every week it ends in disaster."

"Hey," protested Max. "That's not true. They do work. Sometimes."

"Ha!" said Sid. "The last time I helped you I got locked in a smelly old trunk."

Max smirked. "That was a mistake," he said. He had been trying to discover the secret to a really fabulous magic trick so he could be a world-renowned magician. Unfortunately, the false-bottom trunk had ended up tricking them. "It all worked out in the end."

"And the Fresh'n'Tasty catering business?" asked Sid. "You were going to make a fortune supplying cafeterias and hospitals with mouth-watering food, but you didn't even get your recipes past the test kitchen."

"You only had a minor case of food poisoning," Max reminded her. "It could have been worse."

Sid laughed. "Okay, Max. What's your big idea?"

Max crossed his arms. "I'm not sure I want to discuss it with you anymore."

"Come on," said Sid. "You said you needed my help."

Max hesitated, then nodded. "True."

"So?" prodded Sid. "How are you going to get rich this time?"

"Watch," said Max. Grinning, he plunged feet-first down the ladder. Instead of jumping free when he reached the last rung, he started to swing.

Back and forth he swayed, using his body to make the ladder move faster and faster.

The rush of wind against his face reminded him of the summer he'd decided to win an Olympic gold medal in gymnastics in order to rake in product endorsements. That was a winning idea, too, until he fell off the uneven bars and sprained his wrist.

"Zap! Pow!" shouted Max. He swung even harder. "KA-BLAM!" The tree jerked and creaked and a few leaves fluttered to the ground.

"Hey," cried Sid. She clutched the edge of the tree house opening with white-knuckled fingers. "You're going to hurt yourself. Or worse, hurt me!"

"Have no fear," called Max. He swung one last time, did a perfect somersault in the air and landed on the grass. "Max the Mighty Superhero is here!"

3 Distressed Damsel

Sid climbed down the tree house ladder and stared at Max. "Superhero?"

"That's right," Max said in a deep voice. He thrust his chest out, put his hands on his hips, and jutted his chin forward.

Sid's lips twitched.

Max thrust his chest out further.

Sid wrapped her arms around her middle and collapsed on the ground, choking with laughter. "A superhero," she finally gasped. She rolled over to look at Max, wiping tears from the corners of her eyes. "Did you wake up with X-ray vision this morning?"

Max frowned. "Of course not."

"Did you step in a puddle of radioactive waste on your way over?" she asked with a giggle.

"Don't be ridiculous," said Max. He kept his hands on his hips, but let his chest relax. It was starting to ache, anyway. "If you're not going to take me seriously, I'm going home."

Sid dragged herself into a sitting position. "Sorry, Max," she said, "but you have to admit, it sounds insane."

"Not really," said Max. He sat on the grass and leaned forward earnestly. "What do all super-heroes have in common?"

Sid hiccuped. "Tights?"

"For the last time, I'm not wearing tights," cried Max.

Sid gaped at him. "Huh?"

"Never mind," said Max, lowering his voice. At least he had her complete attention now. He took a deep breath and started again.

"The one thing that all superheroes have in common is that they do good deeds," he explained, "which makes people happy. And when people are happy, they like to give rewards. Sometimes big rewards."

Sid looked thoughtful. "That's true. A lady dropped her wallet in our store last week and she was so grateful when Ziggy returned it that she gave him fifty dollars."

"Exactly," said Max. "I need to rescue a few kidnapped babies, maybe save a life or two, and whammo! The reward money will start rolling in."

"I don't have to help you make a tinfoil helmet or anything, do I?" asked Sid.

Max glared at her. "No costume."

"Then what do you need me for?" asked Sid.

"I need a sidekick," explained Max. "You can help me locate people in danger."

Sid didn't look convinced. "It sounds kind of goofy."

"Would you rather weed zucchinis?" asked Max.

Sid jumped to her feet. "Where do we start?"

"Let's try Main Street," suggested Max. "There's bound to be some action there."

Ten minutes later Max and Sid were downtown. Main Street ran from one end of Brooksville to the other, cutting the town in half. The bank, the newspaper office, Bliss and Ziggy's Vegetarian Grocery Store – all the businesses in town were lined up in a neat row. If something interesting was going to happen in Brooksville, it would happen here.

"What are we looking for again?" asked Sid. Max squinted down the street. High-powered binocular vision would come in handy right about now. "Anything unusual," he said. "Suspicious characters, risky situations. Somebody has to be in danger around here somewhere."

Sid nodded doubtfully. "If you say so."

They had only walked a few steps when Max

noticed an elderly woman with heavy bags of groceries waiting near a crosswalk. The light blinked WALK, but the woman didn't cross.

"Crazy cart-wheeling crosswalks!" cried Max. He couldn't believe his luck. A damsel in distress! He darted forward.

"Allow me," he offered gallantly. He grabbed a bag of groceries out of the woman's arms and gripped her elbow firmly. "Right this way, Ma'am."

"Well, thank you, dear, but . . ."

"Oh, I'm happy to help," said Max. Tugging a little, he got the woman off the curb and they started across the street.

"But . . ."

"You really shouldn't be carrying these groceries all by yourself," said Max. A carton of milk and several grapefruits stuck out of the bag he was holding. "You're very lucky I came along." They reached the opposite sidewalk and Max helped her up onto the curb.

"There," he said with a grin. His first act of heroism. Maybe it wasn't as exciting as saving someone from a burning building, but it was a start. "And remember," he added, "if you're ever in trouble, just call. Max is the name and saving people is my game."

"Thanks, dear," said the woman, slightly out of breath. "But I was just waiting for my husband to bring the car around. There he is now," she added, pointing across the street.

Max saw a station wagon pull up to the sidewalk where the woman had been standing. A man with a white moustache got out and looked around, scratching his head.

"Oh," gulped Max. He suddenly wished he had the power of invisibility. "Sorry. I'll help you back."

Sid was still snickering when Max finally got the woman back to her car and handed over the groceries. They continued along Main Street, Sid's face red from laughing and Max's from embarrassment.

"Don't say a word," warned Max. "It was a simple misunderstanding. Could have happened to anyone."

"Oh, sure," giggled Sid. "I can't wait to see who you help next."

4 Unwanted Superhero

Max and Sid walked from one end of Main Street to the other. People smiled and nodded at them. Bliss waved through the front window of her shop and little kids wandered around, giggling and slurping ice-cream cones. No one seemed to need rescuing.

"So much for that," said Sid when they reached the library. It was the last building on Main Street. "Want to catch a movie or something?"

"No way," said Max. He spun around on his heel. "I've got lives to save."

"Come on, Max," groaned Sid. "How long are we going to do this?"

"Sorry," said Max, marching back the way they'd come. His arms swung at his sides. "A superhero's job is never done." He scanned the sidewalks on both sides of the street. Absolutely nothing would escape his notice this time.

Sid rolled her eyes. "Oh, brother."

They walked in silence for a block. Then Max saw something that made the hair on the back of his neck tingle.

"Blistering blue bicycles," he whispered. There was no time to waste. He broke into a run.

"What are you doing?" cried Sid.

Max raced forward, focused on the scene in front of him. Half a block away, a small girl in pigtails pedaled her bicycle downhill toward Main Street. The hill was steep, curving straight into a busy intersection.

Directly ahead, a delivery van approached the intersection, motor grumbling and gears grinding. The traffic light flashed green and the van picked up speed. So did the little girl.

"Stop!" Max shouted, waving his arms as he ran. The little girl looked up, smiled a gap-toothed smile, and waved back.

Max pointed frantically at the van. "Stop! Danger!"

The girl lifted her feet from the pedals and her training wheels blurred. Her pigtails

streamed out behind her. Max glanced at the van, mentally calculated the point of impact, and put on a fresh burst of speed. As the girl neared the sidewalk he dove through the air, arms outstretched, and tackled her. He knocked her off the bike and they crashed to the ground, rolling to a stop against a prickly hedge.

"Oooomph," grunted Max.

"Aaaaaah," screamed the girl.

The van drove by.

"Are you all right?" asked Max. His heart was pounding so fast and loud that it sounded like someone was playing drums between his ears.

The little girl sat up, clutched her knee and glared at Max. "What did you do that for?"

Max stared at her. "What?"

"Look," she cried. Tiny beads of blood formed on her knee where the skin was scraped away. "You big meanie!"

"Hey, I saved your life, kid," retorted Max, climbing to his feet. He dusted grass off his pants and glared back.

"No you didn't," scoffed the girl. "I always stop at the bottom. I've done it a million times."

Sid ran up. "Are you guys okay?"

"No," snapped the little girl. "He hurt my knee. And look at my bike. I'm telling my daddy!"

Sid righted the bicycle. She straightened the front wheel and re-attached the handlebar tassels. "All better," she said. "You don't have to tell your daddy anything. It was an accident."

The little girl jumped up, kicked Max in the shin and hopped back on her bike. She pedaled away with one last dirty look in Max's direction.

"How was I supposed to know she was going to stop?" mumbled Max. He rubbed his shin. "She could have been killed. I'm a hero. I should be rewarded, not kicked."

"Maybe Brooksville doesn't need a super-hero," said Sid. "I'm sorry, Max, but I think your idea is lame."

Max clenched his fists. There was nothing

wrong with his idea. It was a brilliant idea. There just *had* to be someone around here who needed his help.

5 Brooksville's Most Wanted

"You gave it your best shot," said Sid. She put her arm around Max's shoulders and led him away. "Come on, let's go home."

"Home?" repeated Max, surprised. "Why would I want to go home? You saw me, I almost saved that kid's life. I'm getting better at this superhero stuff."

"But I'm hungry," complained Sid. "And your mom makes the best cookies. She never puts weird stuff in them like flax seeds or carob powder. Bliss's cookies could sink ships."

Max hesitated, glancing around. A woman in the Laundromat read a book while clothes spun in the dryer. Next door, two teenagers lounged against the counter in the video store, chatting with the clerk. Nothing out of the ordinary seemed likely to happen today.

"I guess we could try again tomorrow," he said slowly. Then he caught sight of something through the window of the appliance store. His eyes widened. The gears in his brain began to click and spin.

"What is it now?" groaned Sid.

Max stared at a row of televisions. He recognized the program they were showing, even without the sound. It was the one where people turn in bad guys for a reward. The bigger the criminal, the bigger the reward.

"Look," he whispered. "That lady just got money for turning in someone who was on the FBI's Most Wanted list." He turned to Sid. "Lots and lots of money!"

"So?" said Sid.

"Brooksville is probably loaded with people hiding from the law," said Max excitedly. "It's perfect because nobody would ever think to look here."

Sid squinted at Max. "I don't know . . ."

"He could be one," said Max, pointing at a man coming out of the post office with a brown package under his arm. "Or them," he said, gesturing at an elderly couple sitting on a bench, holding hands. "It could be anybody. All we have to do is figure out who is wanted by the law, and turn them in."

"And how are we supposed to do that?" asked Sid with a snort. "We can't just walk up to strangers and ask if they happen to be escaped convicts or something. It's crazy, Max."

"We don't have to ask," said Max. His brain whirled at top speed. People who catch criminals are heroes, too. Pointing out crooks from a safe distance sounded a lot easier than risking life and limb rescuing people. Max rubbed his throbbing shin. A lot less painful, too.

"We need to study some WANTED posters," he said, his eyes shining. "Once we know what the fugitives look like, we can scout around. We recognize someone, tell the police, and collect our reward money. We'll be rich in no time!"

"Where are we going to find these posters?" asked Sid. "This isn't the Wild West, you know."

Max waved away her protests. "I know that, Dippy. We have to go straight to the source."

Sid frowned. "The FBI?"

"No," scoffed Max. He strode purposefully

down the sidewalk. "The police, of course. They must keep a list of this kind of thing. And since I know the local police personally, I'm sure it will be easy to get a look at that list."

Sid scurried to catch up with him. "Are you talking about Officer Todd? Just because you happened to be there when he arrested that jewelry thief . . ."

"I helped him catch that thief," corrected Max. "I'm sure he'll help us."

Max led the way up the police station's front steps and pushed open the gleaming glass doors. Inside, the station was filled with desks and chairs and ringing telephones.

"I'll do the talking," whispered Max.

Sid grunted. "Fine by me."

Max approached the reception desk. A woman wearing a telephone headset looked up and smiled at them.

"I need to talk to Officer Todd," said Max in his most grown up voice. "It's important."

The receptionist wrinkled her brow. "Is it an emergency?"

"Not exactly," said Max, "but it is official police business." He didn't want to lie, but he wanted to be taken seriously.

"I'm sorry, Officer Todd is busy right now," said the receptionist. She passed a pad of yellow paper and a pencil across the desk. "Perhaps you'd like to leave a message?"

"Let's just go," hissed Sid.

Max ignored her and gave the receptionist what he hoped was a charming smile. "Officer Todd and I are old friends. You could even say we're colleagues. We've worked on cases together in the past. In fact, I single-handedly captured . . ."

A tall man wearing a uniform stepped out of a room behind the reception area. "Anne, I need those reports," he said without looking up from the file in his hands. "Where are they?"

"Sorry, sir," the receptionist replied, picking up a stack of papers and holding them out. "They're right here."

"Officer Todd," said Max. He leaned over the desk and thrust out his hand. "Nice to see you."

Officer Todd looked up, startled. His eyes widened when he saw Max.

"Not you again," he groaned.

6 Back to Square One

"Officer Todd, we need to talk," insisted Max.

"I tried to get him to leave a message," said the receptionist.

"That's okay," Officer Todd told her. He rubbed one hand over his short, stubbly hair and studied Max. "I remember you. Persistent sort of kid. You're not going away until we speak, are you?"

Max grinned. "Nope."

"Come in then," said Officer Todd. "Let's get this over with."

Max and Sid stepped past the frowning receptionist and followed Officer Todd into his office. He sat behind a dented metal desk and gestured to two chairs.

"Sit," he said. "Tell me what's on your mind."

"Well," began Max. "We need to look at some mug shots."

Officer Todd leaned forward. "Mug shots? Have you witnessed a crime?"

"No, no," said Max. "It's nothing like that. Sid and I . . ."

"Mostly Max," muttered Sid. She slouched lower in her chair.

"We," continued Max, "have decided to go into the business of identifying and exposing criminals. You know, like on TV. So we need to take a look at your Most Wanted list – check out a few mug shots, maybe take notes on any identifying features, like scars or tattoos or . . ."

Max's voice trailed off. Officer Todd's face was turning an odd shade of purple.

"We'll turn the criminals over to you, of course," Max assured him. "We only want the reward money."

"You want access to confidential police files?" asked Officer Todd in a mild tone that didn't match his pressure-cooker complexion. "Is that all? Perhaps you'd like to borrow a pair of handcuffs. Or why don't I lend you my badge? You know, just in case?"

Max's eyes lit up, then he frowned. "You're making fun of me."

Officer Todd took a deep breath and reached for a mug of coffee sitting on his desk. He took a sip before replying.

"Listen, kid," he said. "This idea of yours is bad news. First of all there aren't any criminals hiding in Brooksville."

"That's what I told him," piped up Sid.

Max glowered at her.

"And secondly," continued Officer Todd, "even if there were criminals hiding in Brooksville, I certainly wouldn't let the two of you run around town spying on them. It would be too dangerous."

"But . . ." Max began.

"Leave the police work to us," said Officer Todd, staring hard at Max with steely gray eyes.

Max scowled. This wasn't going the way he'd hoped.

"That's an order," growled Officer Todd.

"Okay, okay," muttered Max.

"I guess our meeting is over then," said the policeman. He looked at Max and his expression softened. "I'm sorry to burst your bubble, Max.

You're a good kid, but you're going to have to find yourself a different hobby. Something nice and safe."

Max stood up. "I guess you're right. Thanks anyway. Sorry to waste your time."

Officer Todd walked them to the door. "Remember what I said. Criminals aren't nice people. I don't want you getting mixed up in any funny business."

Before they knew it, Max and Sid were standing on the sidewalk in the afternoon sunshine, right back where they started.

"Hey, Max," said Sid, slugging him gently on the arm. "You okay?"

Max smiled. "Of course."

"How about we go check out the cookie situation at your place?" she suggested.

"Sure, why not?" said Max. He looked at the police station one last time then turned in the direction of home. "I always think better on a full stomach."

7 Cookie Crumbs and Classifieds

Max kicked open the kitchen door and leaped to the center of the tiled floor, his hands on his hips. "I'm home," he announced.

Dad looked up from the kitchen table. It was piled high with papers. "Hi, kids."

Sid sniffed the air. "Something smells yummy."

"Help yourself," said Dad, jerking his thumb toward the cookie jar on the counter by the stove. "Mom's at work," he told Max, "but she made her famous oatmeal pecan cookies."

"Great," said Max. He chose a cookie and offered the jar to Sid. Taking a bite, he reviewed his day. What exactly had gone wrong? He swallowed and took another bite, thinking hard.

Sid slipped two cookies into her sweatshirt pocket and took a huge bite of a third. She sighed happily and licked crumbs off her upper lip.

"What's all this, Mr. W?" she asked, pointing at the papers.

Dad frowned and rubbed his temple. "Our copy editor is sick with the flu," he said. "I got stuck putting together the classifieds. I thought I'd get a head start on it now, or I'll never get out of the office tomorrow."

"Looks kind of boring," said Sid.

"Actually," said Dad, "It's more interesting than you'd think. People run the strangest ads." He rummaged through his briefcase and pulled out a piece of flowery pink stationery. "Look at this one. *'Lost: Purple snowshoes. Size XXL'.* How unusual is that?"

"Pretty strange, all right," agreed Sid.

"I've got to sort these into categories," said Dad, waving at the papers and file folders in front of him. "Then check them for spelling errors and . . ."

"Well, good luck, Dad," said Max, sensing a long explanation. "We'll be out back if you need us."

The door banged shut behind them. Max couldn't afford to get caught up in his dad's work. What he needed right now was a new plan, or he could kiss being a superhero goodbye.

Max walked over to the giant hammock slung between two tall evergreens in the far corner of the yard. It was one of his favorite places to think. He sank into the mesh netting and pushed off with one toe.

"Don't feel bad about today," said Sid. She sat cross-legged on the grass nearby and watched him swing back and forth. "At least you tried."

"Uh huh," said Max. Maybe he had been going about this the wrong way. Maybe he needed to start small, then work his way up to bigger things.

"Yoo-hoo," said Sid, frowning. "Are you even listening to me?"

"Mm-hmm," said Max. Starting small was definitely a good idea. But how? If the FBI's Most Wanted list was off limits, what was left? Something Dad had said tickled his brain, but he couldn't quite place it.

"We could dye your hair pink and dress you in an evening gown," suggested Sid. She crossed her arms over her chest and squinted at Max. "What do you think of that?"

"Yeah, sure," said Max. He stared at the clouds with a distant look in his eyes, like he was watching a movie in his head.

Sid cleared her throat nervously. She'd seen

that look before. Usually right before Max got her involved in some whacko scheme. Suddenly weeding the zucchini patch didn't sound so bad after all.

"Well, I should probably go home now," she said, scrambling to her feet.

Max dug his heel into the grass and the hammock stopped swinging. "Shivering super-heroes," he exclaimed. "I've got it!"

Sid swallowed hard. "Got what?"

"The solution," cried Max. "We need to get our hands on another kind of missing persons list."

"Didn't you hear anything Officer Todd said?" asked Sid.

Max focused on Sid's anxious face and smiled. "Sure. He said we couldn't look at confidential police files. So what we need to do is look at some files that aren't so top secret."

"But Max," protested Sid. "Crooks are bad people, remember?"

"I know," said Max with a sly smile. "Officer Todd's quite right. Who wants to mess with criminals anyway? I've got a much, much better idea."

Sid gulped. "What is it?"

"Meet me tomorrow at noon outside the newspaper office," said Max, "And you'll find out."

8 Ticket to Riches

"Okay, I'm here," Sid said the next day. "What's your big idea?"

"I thought I would be a good son and pay Dad a visit at work," said Max, leaning against the newspaper building. He smiled innocently.

Sid pursed her lips, but didn't answer.

A bell chimed above Max's head as he pushed the door open. "Hi, Dad," he called.

The Brooksville Times was a small newspaper located in an even smaller office. The front room was crowded with desks and computers and shelves stuffed full of papers and files.

Dad looked up from his desk. A sharpened pencil stuck out from behind each ear and he was surrounded by sloppy piles of papers. He raised a hand in greeting when he saw Max and Sid.

"What are you kids doing here?" he asked.
Max lifted his shoulders in a casual shrug. "We thought we'd drop by and say hello. Are you busy?"

"Just putting the finishing touches on my latest article," said Dad. He grinned and tapped a piece of paper with a third pencil. "Mr. Perkins discovered a family of badgers in his backyard. This amazing mammal, the largest member of the weasel family, is very ferocious and has been known to kill a dog. Its long, thick fur can even protect it from snakebites. Isn't that fascinating? All I need now is a really great photo. A picture's worth a thousand words, you know, and . . ."

"That's super, Dad," interrupted Max. "So is this week's edition all set to go to the printer?"

Dad blinked. "The printer? Right, of course. Yes, everything is here on my desk." He looked at the disaster zone in front of him and smiled ruefully. "Somewhere."

Across the room a telephone rang.

"Excuse me," Dad said, jumping up from his desk. "I'm the only one here today."

Max slipped behind the desk as soon as Dad left to answer the phone. Keeping one eye on Dad, who had his back to them, Max moved the badger article aside. He flipped through the thick sheaf of papers he found beneath it.

"What are you looking for?" hissed Sid.

"Something special," whispered Max. "It should be around here somewhere . . . ah, here it is."

Max scanned the page. "Zowie," he muttered under his breath. He grabbed a scrap of paper and jotted something down. There was barely enough time to slip the paper into his pocket and put the badger article back before Dad hung up.

"Sorry about that," said Dad. He smiled when he saw Max behind his desk. "Want a job? One of our paper boys just called in sick."

"No thanks," said Max. "I, uh, promised Sid we'd spend the day together. We'd better run, or we'll be late."

"But what about our visit?" called Dad. "I was just about to explain the mating habits of badgers . . ."

The phone rang again.

Max seized the opportunity to escape. "Bye, Dad," he called, dragging Sid out of the newspaper office.

"What was that all about?" demanded Sid, as the door closed behind them.

Max reached into his pants pocket and pulled out the piece of paper. Slowly, he opened his fist until Sid could see what was written on it.

"A telephone number?" asked Sid.

"Not just any telephone number," said Max, holding the paper between two fingers and waving it under Sid's nose. "This number is our ticket to riches."

Sid batted the paper away. "You've lost me."

"Officer Todd told us to stay out of police business, right?" said Max.

Sid nodded.

"But he didn't say anything about staying out of the classifieds, did he?" chortled Max. He looked like the cat that swallowed the canary, and maybe a few parakeets, too.

Sid stared at him blankly. "The classifieds?"

"That's right." Max did a gleeful dance and flapped the scrap of paper above his head. "This is from a lost puppy ad. This guy wants his puppy back a lot. In fact, he wants it so badly that he's . . ."

". . . offered a reward!" finished Sid. "I get it now. But why all the cloak and dagger stuff? Why couldn't you pick up a paper and check out the classifieds like a normal person?"

"Because," explained Max, "The classifieds on Dad's desk are for next week's paper. That means nobody has seen them yet, so we've got a head start. We can find this dog, call the number, and collect the reward money before anyone else even knows it's missing."

"Isn't that cheating?" asked Sid.

Max sniffed. "I prefer to call it using my brain."

Sid groaned. "That brain of yours gets us into more trouble . . ."

"This time," said Max, "I've got the perfect plan!"

9   Lost Puppy Blues

"So how exactly are we going to find this dog?" asked Sid.

Max thought for a moment. He tried to put himself in the lost puppy's shoes. Or paws, rather. Where would he go if he were a pooch?

The butcher shop came to mind. Or maybe the big yellow fire hydrant over on Shirley Avenue. Then he thought of the most obvious place of all.

"To the park!" he cried, pointing east. The park was always chock full of dogs – and picnics and bikes and Frisbees and a hundred other things dogs find irresistible.

Sid sighed, but trotted behind Max as he led the way down a back alley. They jogged away from Main Street, leaving the stores and offices behind.

"What kind of puppy are we looking for, anyway?" asked Sid, six blocks later.

"Chow Chow," wheezed Max. He stopped

and leaned forward, his hands gripping his knees. Too bad he didn't have super-human stamina. Superheroes shouldn't get winded so easily.

"What what?" asked Sid.

To Max's annoyance, Sid didn't seem to be the least bit tired. Must be all that broccoli and wild rice, he thought, gulping a lungful of air.

"A Chow Chow," he explained, breathing a little easier now, "is a Chinese breed of dog with a wrinkly face, a blue tongue, and lots of fur. I bet they cost a fortune, which is perfect. An expensive dog will bring in a higher reward, right?"

"I guess so," said Sid.

Max straightened up and put his hand on Sid's shoulder. "We're almost there. Let's go find that reward money . . . I mean that lost dog."

Together, they searched the park. They looked behind every garbage container, under every bush and park bench, and beside the washrooms and water fountain.

The park was crawling with dogs; big drooling dogs, little yipping dogs, dogs of every shape and size. Unfortunately, every single one was

attached to a leash that was attached to an owner.

"This isn't working," said Sid, peering behind a "Don't Be a Litterbug" sign.

Max's shoulders slumped. Was this idea a bust, too? Maybe Sid was right, and his entire superhero plan really was lame. Suddenly, he stiffened and drew in a sharp breath.

"Look," he hissed.

It was a puppy. A small, fuzzy, wrinkly-faced puppy. And it wasn't wearing a leash.

"Definitely Chow Chow," whispered Max.

"Definitely alone," whispered Sid.

The puppy sat on the opposite bank of a small duck pond. Its round head drooped forlornly and it shivered in spite of the warm afternoon sunshine. Max had never seen anything so pathetic.

"Poor thing," said Sid. "It's lost and scared."

"Not for long," declared Max. He took two steps toward the duck pond, then froze.

A shadowy figure slipped out of the bushes on the opposite bank and sidled up to the puppy. It was an overweight man squeezed into a leather trench coat two sizes too small, with a cowboy hat pulled low over his eyes.

Glancing right, then left, the man bent forward and scooped up the Chow Chow. The puppy's startled yip floated across the water to Max and Sid. Putting one hand over the dog's muzzle, the man slipped the struggling animal under one arm and hurried away.

10 Disappearing Dognappers

"Plundering puppy-snatchers!" cried Max. "Somebody stop him!"

The man glanced up, startled. He quickened his pace, but nobody else paid attention to Max's cry.

Max had to do something, and fast. He dashed forward, forgetting that it was important to watch his step in a park filled with dogs. He took two steps, then one sneaker skidded out from under him and he felt himself falling sideways.

Splash!

"Help," he cried, flopping about in the shallow water. His arms and legs flailed wildly, sending brownish green droplets in every direction. He struggled to sit up, but only sank deeper into the soft, oozing mud that lined the bottom of the pond.

"I'm stuck!" he cried, holding out a slimy hand.

Sid grabbed it and jerked him out. "What kind of superhero steps in dog poo?"

"Never mind that," said Max, wiping algae out of his eyes. "Which way did he go?"

Sid pointed toward a small ice-cream stand. "Up there."

Max broke into a run. His clothes were soggy and heavy, and the sound of his footfalls sloshed inside his skull as he raced up the hill.

Thud, splat. Thud, splat.

Sid raced along beside him. Together, they reached the top of the hill and stopped. The man in the trench coat had vanished.

"Disappearing dognappers!" cried Max. He spun around in a circle. He spotted a woman pushing a baby stroller and two teenagers on in-line skates. No trench coat guy. "Where did he go?"

Sid clutched his arm. "Look! In the parking lot."

Max saw a flash of leather between a minivan and a sports car. Time was running out. If this guy got into his vehicle and drove away, they'd lose him forever.

"Follow me," he whispered to Sid. "We need to get his licence plate number."

They ducked out of sight behind a jeep and moved toward the man, scuttling like crabs between cars. When they were two vehicles away, Max held up his hand in warning. Sid crouched against the pavement and Max peered around a tire.

"Where are my keys?" the man muttered, fumbling in his pocket. He shifted the Chow puppy to his other arm to dig in the pocket of the purple velour tracksuit he wore under his trench coat. The dog whined and squirmed.

"Quiet, you little fleabag," said the man. Max

heard a metallic rattle and the man pulled out a set of keys. "You've been a troublemaker since the day you were born."

Sid tugged the back of Max's shirt. She pointed at the bumper of the man's car. It was an older car, brown with holes in the fenders where the rust had eaten through the metal. The licence plate was smeared with mud. If only I had X-ray vision, thought Max, frustrated.

The man fit a key into the lock and jerked the door open. In a moment, he'd get inside and drive away. The puppy, and the reward, would be lost forever.

Max took a deep breath and stepped out from behind the tire. "Hold it right there," he ordered.

The man froze, the keys dangling from his fingers.

"Step away from the car," said Max in a deep voice.

"Hey, I wasn't doing anything wrong," said the man. He turned around slowly, one hand in the air. "I swear . . ." He stopped when he saw

Max, standing in a puddle of water.

"Is this some kind of joke?" he asked, half-smiling, his beady eyes scanning the parking lot as though he expected someone with a hidden camera to jump out.

Max shook his head. "No joke, Mister. We saw the whole thing." He glanced behind him, but his hiding spot was empty. Sid was gone.

"Get lost, kid," said the man. He plopped the puppy on the front seat and waved Max away with a plump hand.

"I know what you're doing," said Max. "And it's against the law."

The man squinted at Max. His forehead bulged under the rim of his hat, making Max think the hat might pop off at any moment. "What are you talking about?"

Max pointed at the quivering bundle of fur in the car. "That."

The man grunted in surprise and raised a clenched fist, then quickly lowered it as a woman in tennis shorts jogged past. "Mind your own business, kid," he growled, stepping forward.

"Before you get hurt."

Max gulped and backed away. He suddenly felt vulnerable. This man was a puppy-snatcher. Who knew what else he was capable of?

Just then heavy footsteps approached behind Max. "What seems to be the problem?"

11 A Puppy Tale

The man in the trench coat looked over Max's shoulder and his face paled. "There's no problem here, sir."

Officer Todd stepped forward with Sid behind him. She grinned and gave Max the thumbs up sign. Officer Todd, however, wasn't smiling. He laid a heavy hand on Max's damp shoulder. Max's legs, which already felt like wet noodles, threatened to collapse.

"What's going on?" asked Officer Todd. He squeezed Max's shoulder, then frowned. "And what's that awful smell?"

The man snatched his hat off and started talking before Max could say a word. "This pesky kid is following me," he sputtered, spraying the air with a fine mist of spittle. "I'm in quite a hurry, so if it's all right with you, officer, I'll be on my way . . ."

"No!" cried Max. "You can't let him go. He's a criminal!"

"A criminal?" squeaked the man. Beads of sweat broke out on his upper lip. "That's non-sense."

"He's a dognapper," said Max.

"Dognapper?" The man stared at Max, then giggled. Color crept back into his face. "I think you swallowed too much pond water, kid."

"It's true," said Max. He grabbed Officer Todd's arm and yanked him forward. The Chow Chow cowered on the seat behind the steering wheel, watching them through a mask of fur. "He stole that puppy. If you don't believe me, ask Sid."

"Is this your animal?" asked Officer Todd.

The man smiled. "Yes, of course."

"He's lying," insisted Max, still clutching the policeman's sleeve. "The puppy was alone. It has no collar. It was lost, I tell you!"

"How can you be so sure?" asked Officer Todd.

Max hesitated. "I just know."

"Tell him about the ad," hissed Sid.

Officer Todd looked from Sid to Max. "What ad?"

Max let go of the sleeve and stared at his sneakers. Was it a crime to look at the newspaper before it was published? The last thing he wanted to do was get Dad in trouble. "Well, we saw this classified ad, you see, for a lost Chow Chow and . . ."

". . . you were looking to collect the reward," finished Officer Todd. "Gee, that sounds awfully familiar."

"Anyway," said Max, returning to the subject. "We were about to rescue the puppy when this guy came along and snatched it. In broad daylight!"

Officer Todd thought for a moment. "He could have seen the same ad you did."

Max gulped. How was he going to explain that the ad hadn't even hit the newsstands yet?

"It was my ad," said the man. "My name is Arthur Quimbly and my puppy ran away two days ago. I've been worried sick. She's like family to me, she's all I've got."

"Where's her collar?" challenged Max.

"I took it off to give her a bath the day she

ran away," explained Quimbly. He turned back to Officer Todd. "Wait, I can prove it."

He reached into his car and produced a sheaf of flyers off the dash. Above the word "LOST" was a blow-up photo of the Chow Chow. Beneath it, in smaller type, was Quimbly's name and a phone number. Max didn't need to look at the scrap of paper in his pocket to know that it was the same number.

"I think you owe this man an apology," said Officer Todd. His gaze bored into Max like a jack-hammer. "Now, Max."

"Uh, sorry," stammered Max. He stared at Quimbly, who clutched his hat in one hand, and the flyers in the other. "I guess I made a mistake."

"Whatever," said Quimbly. "Am I free to leave now?"

"Certainly." Officer Todd nodded. "Sorry for the misunderstanding."

Max watched as Quimbly got into his car and drove away. Why had he been so furtive in the park? And why did he act so nervous when Officer Todd showed up? It was like he had something to hide.

"Max," said Officer Todd, jerking Max out of his thoughts. "I thought I warned you about this yesterday."

"You said to stay away from dangerous criminals . . ." began Max.

"You're lucky I happened to be driving past and your friend Sid, here, flagged me down," the officer interrupted. "Most people don't take kindly to being accused of stealing. Especially of stealing their own animals."

Max tried again. "But the puppy was scared of him . . ."

"I'm a patient man," said Officer Todd. A bulging vein in his neck made Max doubt his words. "But this is not to happen again. Do you understand?"

"But . . ."

Officer Todd repeated his question, spacing it out so that each word was crystal clear. "Do . . . you . . . understand?"

Max's shoulders sagged. "Yes, sir."

Officer Todd stared at him for a moment. Then he nodded. "Good."

Max watched Officer Todd stride back to his car. As soon as the patrol car drove out of sight, he sighed deeply and thrust his hands into his pockets.

"That's it," he said. "My career as a superhero is officially over."

12 **An Alternate Route**

Sid stared at Max. "You're giving up?" she asked.

Max shrugged and started walking. "What choice do I have?" he said. "You heard Officer Todd. No more chasing bad guys. Period."

Sid caught up to him. She put her arm over his shoulder. "Let's do something else, then. Wanna track down some big purple snowshoes?"

Max shook his head. "Nah. I don't feel like it."

"Well, I sure don't feel like pulling weeds today." Sid thought for a moment. "Let's catch that movie now."

"No money," said Max. "Remember?"

"Ask your dad to lend you some," suggested Sid.

"He never just *lends* me money," said Max, watching the toes of his sneakers on the sidewalk. "He always makes me earn it. You know, by doing odd jobs or whatever."

"Like a paper route?" asked Sid with a small smile.

Max glanced up and groaned. "Exactly."

Sid grabbed Max's arm. "Oh, come on. It won't kill you to earn money in an ordinary way for once."

"You don't get rich by delivering papers," grumbled Max.

"No," agreed Sid. "But you can get enough money for movie tickets. Are you coming?"

Max hesitated, then shrugged and changed direction. "Fine," he muttered. "But don't blame me if this turns out to be the most boring job in the world."

Max's dad was thrilled to see them. "You've come to help?" he asked, his eyes wide with surprise. "Really?"

"We need money to go to the movies later," explained Sid.

"What about your other plans?" asked Dad.

"They didn't exactly work out," mumbled Max.

Dad clapped his hand on Max's shoulder.

"Wonderful! I thought I was going to have to deliver those papers myself. Just for that, I'll throw in extra popcorn money. How does that sound?"

"Yummy," said Sid.

Even Max smiled. "Thanks, Dad."

"Okay, then," said Dad, getting down to business. He handed them a paper. "Here's the route. Follow it closely, every house on the list gets a paper. The carrier bags and the newspapers are out back. Any questions?"

Max and Sid shook their heads.

"Great," said Dad, picking up the telephone. "See you back here in a few hours."

"A few hours?" cried Max. But Dad was already dialing. Max glared at Sid. "I can't believe I let you talk me into this."

They found the canvas bags and filled them with newspapers. Max grunted under the weight. How could paper be so heavy? Together, they stumbled outside and consulted the list.

"This way," decided Max, pointing left. "You take one side of the street and I'll take the other."

An hour later they were both hot and sweaty

and tired. The sun blazed down on them out of the afternoon sky. Max's throwing arm throbbed. Sid had black newsprint smudged across her cheek.

"Water," croaked Max. "Why didn't we bring water?"

Sid grunted and fell on the grass beside the sidewalk. Max let his carrier bag slide off his shoulder and sank down beside her.

"We must be almost done," he said, pulling the wrinkled subscription list out of his pocket. He wiped the sweat out of his eyes so he could see.

Sid groaned and rolled over. "I should have stuck with the zucchinis," she said.

"You were the one who thought manual labor would be a fun way to earn money," Max complained. "I wanted to be a superhero, remember?"

"Yeah, yeah," said Sid. "I know."

"There are only four deliveries left. And they're all on Ramsay Road."

Ramsay Road was on the outer limits of town, where the houses were older and spaced farther apart. Max and Sid walked along the side-walk, reading off the numbers.

"101," said Max, throwing a newspaper onto the front step.

"104, and 106," said Sid, crossing the street to toss two more papers.

"107," said Max, reaching for his last paper. He pulled his arm back to throw it, then froze.

The car in front of 107 Ramsay Road was brown, with rusty fenders. And the licence plate was covered with mud.

"Quimbly," hissed Max.

13 Yips and Yelps

Sid ran back across the street. "Why did you stop?" she asked.

Wordlessly, Max pointed at Quimbly's car.

"What's he doing here?" gasped Sid.

"He put that ad in the classifieds," said Max, thinking aloud. "It makes sense that he'd have a sub-scription."

"Well, deliver the paper, already, and let's get out of here," said Sid. "If Officer Todd catches us here he'll think we're disobeying him."

Max stared at the house. It was a plain two-storey red brick building. The only thing that made it differ-ent from every other house in the neighborhood was a high fence that surrounded the backyard. A super high fence. The highest fence Max had ever seen.

"Come on," urged Sid. "Throw the paper."

Max started up the front walk.

"What are you doing?" hissed Sid.

"My job, of course," said Max. "What do you think?"

Sid scurried up the walk behind him. "I think you're spying on Quimbly," she said. "And I also think you're asking for trouble."

Max smiled innocently. "I'm simply hand-delivering this paper. No harm in that."

They reached the front door and Max placed the rolled-up Brooksville Times in the empty letterbox. The front step was bare, no flowerpots or personal knickknacks to give it any personality. A narrow cement path branched off the main walk and curved around the house to a gate in the fence. Max glanced around, then put one foot on the side path.

"What are you doing?" whispered Sid.

Max wasn't sure. All he knew was that there was something weird about that fence. His super-hero warning sensors were tingling.

"Let's get out of here," said Sid. She grabbed Max's elbow. "Right now, before someone notices us."

"Wait," said Max, shaking her off.

"There's no time to wait," said Sid. "Quimbly

could come out at any moment."

"No," said Max. "I mean listen." He tilted his head slightly. "Did you hear that?"

The sound came again, muffled through the thick wooden fence. It was faint, but it was definitely the sound of a dog whining.

"The Chow Chow," cried Sid. Forgetting about Quimbly, she dashed down the path and pressed her ear against the fence. "Max! I heard it again."

The dog gave a halfhearted howl, which turned into a pathetic whimper.

"Do you think she's hurt?" asked Sid.

Max shrugged. The fence was too high to climb and he didn't see any knotholes to peer through.

He tried whistling. "Here, girl."

There was silence, then a tentative bark.

"Come on. Come over to the fence," called Sid. She turned to Max. "She sounds hungry."

"I wish we had some dog treats," said Max.

Sid's eyes lit up. She thrust her hands into her sweatshirt pocket and pulled out a slightly flattened oatmeal pecan cookie.

"Ew," said Max, wrinkling his nose. "You kept that in your pocket overnight?"

Sid brushed off a fuzz ball. "Yeah, so? Bliss doesn't believe in using processed sugar. You ever try eating brownies sweetened with powdered figs?"

Max grimaced and shook his head. He took the squashed cookie and fired it into the air. It smacked against the top of the fence then fell back in the grass at his feet.

"Try again," urged Sid.

Max picked it up and backed up a few steps. He drew his arm back and threw as high and as hard as he could. The oatmeal missile sailed over the top of the fence and into the backyard. They heard a puppy bark. It barked and barked and barked.

"Noisy little thing, isn't she?" said Sid, glancing nervously at the neighboring houses as the barking grew louder.

"That's not one dog," said Max. He turned to Sid. "That sounds like two or three. Maybe more."

Yips and yelps filled the air. "You're right," agreed Sid.

Max remembered something. "Quimbly said he only had one dog, but it sounds like he's got a whole litter in there. Why did he lie?"

"I don't know," said Sid. Her eyes widened at the sound of the front door opening. "But here he comes!"

14 Return of the Superhero

"Hide!" cried Max, diving behind a lilac hedge. Sid was right behind him. With trembling fingers they pushed aside the leafy branches. To their horror, Quimbly waddled down the path straight toward them.

"I've had it with you," shouted Quimbly. "You've caused me enough trouble today."

Sid gasped. Max's hand shot out and covered her mouth. They watched, terrified, as Quimbly stopped three steps away.

"Quit that barking!" he shrieked, banging on the padlocked gate. "Or you'll have the old lady next door over here complaining again. Now knock it off!"

The barking stopped immediately.

"Don't make me come out here again," he warned. Muttering under his breath, he waddled back to the front door and disappeared inside the house.

Sid turned to Max. "Those poor animals,"

she whispered. "How can he talk to them like that?"

"There's something strange going on here," said Max. "We need to find out what it is."

"How?" asked Sid. She pointed at the gate. "You don't happen to know how to pick a lock, do you?"

Max smiled weakly. "I'm a superhero, not a cat burglar."

Sid struggled free of the hedge. "Then that's it, I guess."

"We've got to do something," insisted Max, crawling out behind her. He pulled a twig out of his hair, thinking hard. As a superhero, he was bound to come to the aid of anybody in need. And those dogs were definitely in need. "Let's scope out the perimeter."

Sid frowned. "The what?"

Max sighed and moved forward, still on his hands and knees. "The fence. The puppy ran away, right? It must have escaped somehow."

Max and Sid worked their way along one side of the yard. The fence blocked Quimbly's view of them from the house. As long as the neighbors didn't notice them crawling around like preschoolers in a sandbox, they were safe.

They rounded a corner and started along the back end of the yard. Max stopped.

"Hopping hole-diggers," he whispered. Ahead was a small mound of loose dirt piled against the base of the fence. "The puppy dug a tunnel under the fence. That's how it escaped."

They crawled faster. Max reached it first.

"Oh, no," he said, pounding the soft earth with his fist. The hole had been clumsily boarded up with old pieces of lumber.

"Wait," said Sid. She pointed to a crack in the boards. "Quimbly's a lousy carpenter."

Max slipped off his carrier bag and tossed it aside. While Sid did the same, Max lay flat on the ground and pressed his eye to the small opening and peered into the backyard. His body stiffened. He pulled away, but put a warning hand on Sid's shoulder when she leaned forward to take a look.

"It's pretty bad," he told her.

When Sid moved away from the peephole her face was so pale that her freckles looked like they'd been dabbed on with a brown magic marker. "It's horrible," she whispered.

Max nodded and swallowed hard. Through the gap he'd seen chicken wire and overturned feeding dishes. There wasn't a blade of grass or chew toy in sight. A row of cramped, dilapidated kennels lined one end of the yard. And locked in those cages were puppies. Lots and lots of puppies.

"That's a puppy mill," said Sid in a hoarse voice. "I heard Bliss and Ziggy talking about them once. Dogs are kept in terrible conditions, bred over and over again, then the puppies are sold for lots of money. It's awful, it's inhumane, and I'm sure it's against the law."

"We've got to help them," said Max. "Let's go tell Officer Todd. He'll listen to us . . ."

Sid frowned.

Max broke off, mid-sentence. Sid was right. He was probably the last person Officer Todd would listen to right now. He'd already accused Quimbly of dognapping. There was no way Officer Todd would take Max's word over Quimbly's.

"We need proof," he decided. His brain buzzed, softly at first, then full blast as a solution hit him. He turned to Sid excitedly. "Remember what Dad said?"

Sid shook her head. "Something about badgers being good diggers . . . but even if we could catch one of Mr. Perkins' badgers and bring it out here, there's no way it could dig another hole under the fence before Quimbly noticed us."

"No, no, no," said Max. He jumped to his feet. "He said a picture's worth a thousand words, right? We'll get a picture of this puppy mill. Then we'll have all the proof we need to put Quimbly behind bars, where he belongs."

15 Fenced In

Max leaned against the fence beside the boarded up hole and brainstormed out loud.

"I could use Dad's camera," he suggested. "It's got a zoom lens and everything. He's even got it loaded with special low-light film because badgers are nocturnal and he wants to take a bunch of pictures of them."

Sid squinted at him. "Why would you need low-light film?"

"For night photography, of course," said Max, his brain spinning at whirlwind speed. "I could sneak out of the house after dark, once Mom and Dad are asleep, then come get you. We'd need a special signal. I could throw pebbles at your bedroom window, or maybe hoot three times like an owl . . ."

"Whoa," cried Sid. "Hold on!" She crossed her arms over her chest and glared at Max. "There's absolutely no way I'm sneaking around town in the middle of the night. We've got school tomorrow. And what if we get caught? We'd be grounded for a year!"

"But I swore an oath to uphold justice for all by deciding to become a superhero," Max told her. "Those puppies need us."

"You're the superhero, not me," snapped Sid. She thought for a moment, then sighed. "But you're right. Somebody has to close that puppy mill."

"Right," said Max. He rubbed his hands together happily. "I'll pick you up at midnight. Wear black."

"Forget it," snapped Sid. "This time, we're using my plan."

Max's mouth fell open. "You have a plan?"

"Don't look so surprised," muttered Sid. "Just because I run all over town helping you with your crazy ideas doesn't mean I don't have a few of my own."

Max grinned. "Shoot."

"We have to tell Ziggy," Sid decided.

Max raised one eyebrow. "Ziggy?"

Sid shot him a sharp look. "Yes, Ziggy. He may act goofy sometimes, but he's been fighting animal cruelty since I was a baby. He's even the president of some kind of animal rights organization. He once handcuffed himself to a tree to protect the habitat of an endangered bird, you know," she added proudly.

Max nodded reluctantly. "I guess that makes more sense than sneaking out of the house at midnight," he said. "Are you sure you don't want to try scaling the fence first? We could tie our carrier bags together and loop them over the top of the fence and I could stand on your shoulders and . . ."

"We're telling Ziggy," said Sid. "He'll know exactly what to do about Quimbly."

"Fine," grumbled Max. "But a real superhero would . . ."

". . . save the puppies," finished Sid. "And that's what we're going to do. With Ziggy's help."

Max gave up. "Okay, we'll do it your way. Let's get out of here before Quimbly comes back."

"Yeah," agreed Sid. "He gives me the creeps."

They ran in an awkward half-crouch along the fence, heading toward Quimbly's front yard. Hearing their movements, the dogs grew excited.

They barked. And barked and barked.

They'd make good guard dogs, thought Max as he reached the end of the fence. Only a few more steps and they'd be back on Ramsay Road.

Together, they dashed around the corner of the fence and barreled into a plump, purple velour wall. Max gulped and looked up.

It was Quimbly.

16   *Quick-Cash Quimbly*

A pudgy, hairy arm shot out and grabbed Max by the front of the shirt. Another pudgy, hairy arm grabbed Sid. The arms lifted them higher and higher until only their toes touched the ground.

"You again," said Quimbly, breathing in Max's face. He smelled of hard-boiled eggs. "What are you doing snooping around my house?"

"Uh, well," began Max, but his mind was a blank.

"We, er . . ." tried Sid.

"You're spying on me," accused Quimbly.

"Spying?" squeaked Max. "Who, us? No way, we weren't spying on you, we don't know anything about the puppies . . ."

Sid kicked Max.

"I mean," said Max, "We didn't . . ."

"You're trying to get me in trouble with that cop pal of yours," said Quimbly. He tightened his grip on Max's shirt.

"No, no," gurgled Max. "Officer Todd doesn't even know we're here."

Quimbly's expression grew sly. "He doesn't?"

"But our parents do," said Sid, glaring at Max.

"In fact, Max's dad is expecting us back at the newspaper office. He knows exactly which paper route we're working on . . ."

"Paper route, huh?" Quimbly scrutinized them. "Do you carry the papers in your teeth?" Max realized, too late, that they'd left their carrier bags on the ground by the back fence.

Quimbly giggled. The sound was high-pitched and unpleasant. "I think you're lying," he said. "I'll bet nobody even knows you're here."

Max's stomach lurched. What would Quimbly do to them? Lock them up with the puppies? Or worse?

"Nosey, interfering kids," muttered Quimbly.

Before they realized what was happening, Quimbly pinned them against the fence with one arm and began spinning the combination lock on the gate. Max struggled, but it was useless.

Suddenly, the sound of screeching tires filled the air.

"Freeze!" ordered a booming voice. "Back away from the children and keep your hands where I can see them."

Max squinted into the sunlight. "Officer Todd?"

A car door slammed and Officer Todd

approached them. He stood between Quimbly and the children, his hands on his hips. Relief flooded Max's body. In that instant, he knew he was looking at a real superhero. Cape or no cape, Officer Todd was the bravest man he knew.

"I received a report of a disturbance," Officer Todd said, frowning. "I certainly didn't expect to see you two. Again."

Max realized that the neighbor's curtains were pulled back. A woman in hair curlers stuck her head through the open window.

"I told you I'd call the police, Arthur," she shouted in a nasal voice. "I've had it up to here with those noisy dogs of yours. How can I watch my soaps with all that barking?"

"Thank you, Ma'am," said Officer Todd, tipping his hat. "I'll take it from here."

Max gulped when Officer Todd turned expectantly to him. "I can explain," he said quickly. "We wanted to call you first, but we knew you wouldn't believe us. Quimbly really is a criminal. He's running a puppy mill in his backyard!"

Officer Todd stared hard at Max. "Are you telling me that you seriously believe this man is mistreating animals?"

Max nodded.

Officer Todd turned to Quimbly. "What do you say about that, sir?"

Quimbly opened and closed his mouth several times, but nothing came out. Finally he stammered, "This is the second time today these kids have harassed me. I'm a responsible pet owner. They're the ones breaking the law. Trespassing! Vandalism! Slander! I'm going to press charges this time . . ."

Officer Todd held up his hand, signaling for silence. "Let's just calm down," he said. "Why don't you unlock that gate and we'll clear this whole thing up."

Quimbly's lower lip quivered. To everyone's surprise, his shoulders began to shake.

"So my dog has lots of puppies," he blubbered. "Is that a crime? I take care of them the best I can, and sometimes I sell them to make ends meet. Dog food is so expensive . . ."

"And you were looking to make a little quick cash," interrupted Officer Todd. He scowled and shook his head. "When will folks realize that there is no such thing as an easy buck?"

Sid glanced at Max. He swallowed hard and looked away.

"Let's talk about this at the station," said

Officer Todd, leading the sobbing man into the patrol car. He radioed ahead and both Max and Sid's parents were waiting when they walked into the police station.

"Max, honey, are you all right?" cried Max's mom. She hugged Max tightly, pressing his nose into her shoulder.

"I'm fine," Max assured her. He pulled away and grinned at Dad. "But boy, have I ever got a story for you!"

17 Looking for Dollar Signs

The daring rescue made headline news in the Brooksville Times. Max and Sid were treated like heroes. People stopped them in the street asking for autographs and they got free sundaes at the ice-cream shop.

Then one day a letter came from the Brooksville Rescue Abused Animals Taskforce, addressed to Max.

"I knew it," cried Max. "My reward money!"

He ripped open the envelope. "Dear Maximillian J. Wigglesworth III," he read. "We heard of your recent accomplishment and, along with the Mayor of Brooksville, would like to invite you to a special ceremony in your honor."

Max skipped ahead, looking for dollar signs. Then he shrugged. "I guess they want to give it to me in person."

A few days later, Dad drove Max and Sid to the meeting.

The Mayor stood at the front of the room,

distinguished in her official mayoral robes. Beside her stood Ziggy, in carefully pressed blue jeans and a patterned shirt that read, "Honk if You Love Hippos". In his hand was a scuffed briefcase.

The Mayor began the meeting with a speech. It was long and flowery and Max found himself staring at the briefcase. He wondered if it was filled with cash or if he was going to receive a check. Either one was fine with him.

"So, it gives me great pleasure," concluded the Mayor, "to introduce the President of the Brooksville Rescue Abused Animals Taskforce, Mr. Ziggy Stubberfield."

"Thank you," said Ziggy, taking the micro-phone. "These kids are heroes. Not only did they save the lives of some sadly mistreated animals, they helped prevent the same kind of thing from happening again and again in the future. Every puppy mill we shut down brings us one step closer to our goal of protecting animal rights."

The room filled with applause.

"So, it's my extreme privilege," he said, "to present Serendipity Sunshine Stubberfield . . ."

Sid groaned.

". . . and Maximillian J. Wigglesworth III with this commemorative plaque."

Max looked at the wooden plaque and felt like groaning, too.

"And," continued Ziggy, taking a deep breath.

Max felt his hopes rise.

"From this moment on these two young people are honorary members of our organization." Ziggy grinned and clapped along with the audience.

Max forced himself to follow Sid to the front and accept the plaque even though his reward money was flying out the window.

The Mayor approached the microphone. "So how does it feel to be an honorary B.R.A.A.T?"

Max sighed, then smiled. "Wonderful." They had helped shut down the puppy mill. Reward or no reward, he had to admit it did feel wonderful.

The Mayor beamed and laid a ring-covered hand on his shoulder. "Brooksville needs more young people like you. Perhaps some day you'll be Mayor," she added with a laugh.

Max nodded and stared at the golden mayoral chain that hung around her neck. The heavy links glittered in the light.

He glanced around the office. The windows were covered with silk drapes, a Persian carpet lay on the floor and expensive-looking artwork was scattered about the room.

His brain began to buzz. Didn't the Mayor drive a sleek black sports car? And live in the fanciest house in the whole town? Max bet it even had a pool.

"Max?" whispered Sid.

Sid could be his campaign manager. They'd plaster the town with billboards. There would be television debates and private jets and press parties with champagne and caviar and . . .

"Max!" Sid nudged him. "Shake her hand, already."

"Huh?" Max came back into the present. With a grin, he shook the Mayor's hand, then turned to the crowd and waved. "Thank you all for this great honor. And don't forget," he added with a wide grin, "vote Max!"

Check out Max's other exciting adventures – now available with all new illustrations!

MAX THE MAGNIFICENT
978-1-897073-94-0

Determined to become a millionaire by age twelve, Max goes under-cover in the world of magic to discover the one trick that will lead him to riches.

MAX THE MOVIE DIRECTOR
978-1-897073-96-4

Max thinks that he can make his millions if he directs the biggest blockbuster movie of all time. Will his Hollywood ending be jeopardized by one last plot twist?

MAX THE BUSINESSMAN
978-1-897073-93-3

Max is planning to corner the Main Street flower market, until some-one murders "Victor" – a prize-winning orchid. In a flash, Max goes from gardener to detective as he tries to catch the culprit and snag a big reward in the process!